THE
SLEEPING
BEAUTY

THE
SLEEPING
BEAUTY

RETOLD BY
JANE YOLEN

ILLUSTRATED BY
RUTH SANDERSON

ARIEL BOOKS / ALFRED A. KNOPF NEW YORK 1986

To David

J.Y.

To Ken

R.S.

THIS IS A BORZOI BOOK
PUBLISHED BY ALFRED A. KNOPF, INC.

Copyright © 1986 by The Tempest Company
All rights reserved under International and Pan-American Copyright
Conventions. Published in the United States by Alfred A. Knopf, Inc., New York,
and simultaneously in Canada by Random House of Canada Limited, Toronto.
Distributed by Random House, Inc., New York.

Library of Congress Cataloging-in-Publication Data

Yolen, Jane.   The Sleeping Beauty.

Summary: Enraged at not being invited to the princess's christening, the wicked
fairy casts a spell that dooms the princess to sleep for 100 years.
[1. Fairy tales. 2. Folklore] I. Sanderson, Ruth, ill. II. Sleeping Beauty. English.
III. Title.
PZ8.Y78Sk 1986   398.2'1'0924 [E]   86-45374
ISBN 0-394-55431-0

Manufactured in Italy
FIRST EDITION

THE
SLEEPING
BEAUTY

Once upon a time there lived a King and Queen who wanted only one thing—to have a child. But year in and year out the royal cradle stood empty.

One day the Queen and her maidens were bathing in a forest pool. Suddenly a Wise Fairy appeared at the water's edge and said to her, "O Queen, before another summer comes you shall bear a child."

The prophecy came true. In the spring the Queen gave birth to a girl with a crown of red hair and a face as lovely as a flower. Overjoyed, the King named her Briar Rose and planned a great feast in her honor.

He invited his relatives, his friends, and the nobility from near and far. He also sent invitations to the Twelve Wise Fairies to thank them for the prophecy. He had a golden goblet encrusted with jewels made for each of them, twelve goblets in all. But the King had forgotten the thirteenth Fairy, old and ill-tempered, for it was said that she was long dead. However, she was very much alive, and dwelt in a dark tower on the forest's edge, ready to take offense at the slightest insult and pay back any imagined injury with a wicked spell.

The many guests filled the great hall with laughter and song. When the meal was done, each of the Wise Fairies stood to give a magic gift to the little princess. One gave her virtue, another beauty, a third a truthful tongue. And so it went until Briar Rose had everything in the world she might want.

When eleven of the Fairies had given their gifts, there was a sudden banging at the door and the thirteenth Fairy stormed in. She said not a word of greeting but cried out in a voice full of rage: "My gift is a curse: When the child is fifteen years old, she shall prick her finger on a spindle and drop down dead."

Then, muttering angrily, she marched from the room.

The hall fell silent except for the weeping Queen. At last the twelfth Fairy, who had been hiding behind a curtain, crept out. "I have not yet given my wish," she said. "And though I cannot undo my sister's curse completely, I *can* soften it. The princess shall not die. She shall fall into a sleep that lasts one hundred years. At the end of that time a prince will come and wake her."

In the days that followed, the King made a law forbidding anyone in his kingdom to own a spindle. He had a great bonfire set in the castle courtyard into which all the spinning wheels in the land were thrown. He watched the fire until it had burned down to ashes, and only then was he content.

The years passed swiftly and Briar Rose grew into all the gifts the Fairies had given her. She was beautiful, truthful, merry, modest, and wise. Everyone in the kingdom loved her, and because they all loved her and remembered the thirteenth Fairy's curse, no one dared to keep a spindle or wheel within the kingdom's borders.

On the day the princess turned fifteen, her parents planned a great birthday feast. Everyone was so busy preparing for it, they left Briar Rose alone for the first time in her life. Having nothing else to do, she began exploring all the parts of the castle where she had never been before.

As she poked into abandoned pantries and passed through long-forsaken halls, she felt herself drawn towards the dustiest of the chambers, where spiders spun their elusive dreams. At last, behind a heavy brocaded tapestry, she discovered a narrow winding staircase and for some reason felt she had to find out what lay at the top.

The stairs went round and round and up and up until she was dizzy with climbing and afraid to look back down. But she continued, for she was determined to find where the stairs led. At the top was a wooden door, and by the light of a window she could see a rusty key in the lock.

Briar Rose turned the key, expecting it to make a loud,
protesting creak; but to her surprise the door sprang open
without a sound. In the room was a strange old woman sitting
on a stool in front of a large wheel.

"Good day, Granny," said Briar Rose. "Who are you and
what are you doing?" For she had never seen a wheel or spindle.

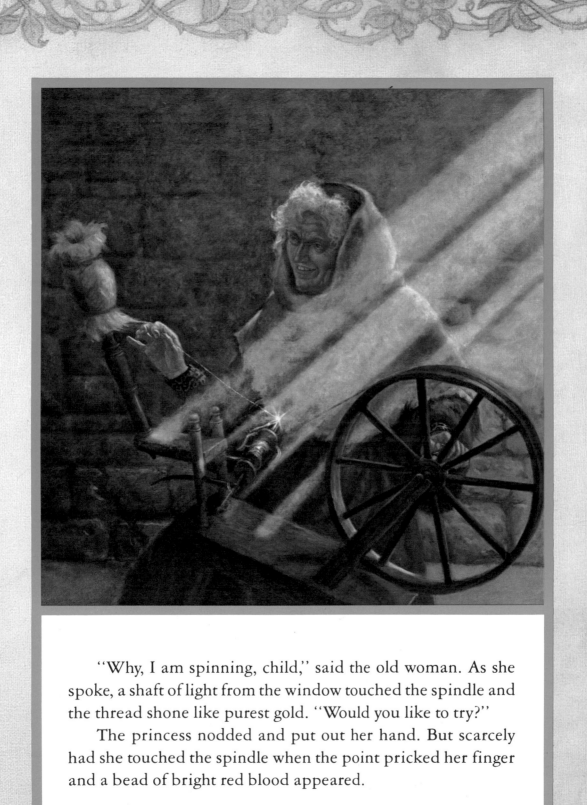

"Why, I am spinning, child," said the old woman. As she spoke, a shaft of light from the window touched the spindle and the thread shone like purest gold. "Would you like to try?"

The princess nodded and put out her hand. But scarcely had she touched the spindle when the point pricked her finger and a bead of bright red blood appeared.

The pain of it was sudden and sharp and Briar Rose felt faint. She opened her mouth to cry out but she could only yawn, overcome with a strange sleepiness. Her eyelids felt so heavy she could not keep them open.

"I am so tired," she said. "May I sit here for a moment?"

The only answer to her question was a high wicked laugh. Briar Rose opened her eyes and looked around the dusty room, but the old spinner had disappeared. And, where the wheel, spindle, and stool had been, there was now nothing but a poor straw pallet.

Sighing, the princess lay down on the straw bed and fell at once into a deep and untroubled sleep. As she slept, the musty room began to change. Draperies of the richest brocades appeared over the bed. The finest satin sheets slipped themselves under her. And pillows bound in ribbons of silk plumped beneath her head.

As Briar Rose slipped even deeper into her magical slumber, the same enchantment crept like a cloud throughout the rest of the castle. The Queen, who had been listening to a song composed especially for the birthday feast, fell fast asleep. And the jester, in the midst of his melody, slept just as soundly.

The King in his great hall, surrounded by snoring courtiers, slept. The ministers in the midst of their meetings slept. The

fire flaming in the kitchen hearth grew quiet, the roast left off its sizzling, and the cook, who was just going to punish the scullery boy for spoiling the sauce, fell asleep before she could give him a slap.

Horses in the stable slept, dogs in the yard, doves on the roof, rats in their hideyholes, flies on the wall, all, all slept. The wind fell, and on the trees in front of the castle not a leaf moved. It was as if death itself had claimed them.

No sooner had everyone fallen asleep than a thorny hedge began to grow around the castle. Within hours it was as high as a man; within days it covered the stone walls. Briary fingers caught on the window ledges and brambles sealed the doors. Each year the hedge crept higher and higher until all that could be seen were the tops of the towers where, in the highest room of all, Briar Rose slept on.

But if the castle could not be seen, stories about the sleeping beauty were heard throughout the countryside. And so one by one by one the sons of kings came to gaze at the enchanted thorns and to dream of the girl who lay asleep in the high tower beyond. Some even tried to fight their way through the hedge, but the deadly briars held them fast.

When none of the kings' sons returned, a darker legend sprang up. The castle was said to be a place of evil, and the sleep therein the sleep of death.

One spring day, many many years later, a prince came riding towards the castle, for he had dreamed of such a place every night the past year. He happened upon an old farmer walking along the road.

"Why is it so desolate here?" asked the prince.

"It is because of the castle and the curse,"

the man replied, and he told the prince the story of the sleeping beauty.

Amazed, the prince said, "But that is what I have dreamed each night for a year: of an ancient castle and a princess asleep in a tall tower. Can you show me the way through the hedge?"

"There is no way," said the old man, shuddering.
"Then I shall make one," said the prince,
"for I must try to see this Briar Rose,
even if it means
my death."

He climbed off his horse and advanced toward the hedge. It was then that he saw why the place had such an evil name, for the briars held fast to whitened bones and to the tatters of royal cloaks.

"How horrible," thought the prince. But he reached out his hand to the hedge nonetheless, for the dream was still strong within him.

Now the prince had no way of knowing it, but exactly one hundred years had passed since Briar Rose had climbed to the tower on her birthday, pricked her finger on a spindle, and fallen into her enchanted sleep. So the moment he touched the first thorn, the briars turned into blossoms that magically parted before him, and he passed through the fierce brambles without so much as a scratch.

He walked and walked through the parting briars until at last he could see the castle ahead of him, with its turrets and parapets and the great vine-covered tower. He went swiftly through the gates and came into the yard, where there were horses and dogs and stableboys asleep on their feet. He glanced at them quickly and walked on.

Inside, the castle was like a tomb, silent and still, and the pall of enchantment lay over all. The only sounds were the prince's steps as he strode through the castle halls. He saw guards asleep with spears in hand, and the King asleep in his great chair. He saw sleeping courtiers and cooks, scullions and sentinels, but he did not see the princess Briar Rose.

The prince searched through every room in the castle, but none of them matched the room of his dreams. He glanced into abandoned pantries and down long-forsaken hallways.

The only signs of life in the castle were his own echoing steps and each deep breath he drew.

At last, behind a heavy tapestry, he discovered a narrow winding staircase. He mounted the steps two at a time and at the top saw a door slightly ajar. Slipping into the room, he found a bed hung with brocades. In its center, on satin sheets, lay a girl with a face as lovely as a flower.

The prince put his hand to his heart and for a moment could not breathe, for she was even more beautiful than in his dream. Slowly, as if he were himself asleep, he touched her hair. Then he leaned down and kissed her gently on the mouth.

She smiled sweetly and opened her eyes. "Oh," she said, "I have been waiting for you for a long, long time."

At her voice, the castle trembled as if awaking. The prince helped her from the bed and it disappeared the moment she stood, but neither of them noticed.

Hand in hand they descended the narrow stairs, where it was so close two could barely pass. When they came to the great stairs, there was the King waiting below to greet them: And though there was room for more than two on that stair, they

stayed close together, their fingers laced like briars in a hedge.

In the courtyard the horses shook their heads and the boys began to brush them. In the Queen's chamber the jester yawned and finished his song. The kitchen fire flickered, the meat sizzled merrily on the spit, and the cook gave the scullery boy such a whack with the spoon he yelled right out loud.

So the prince and
Briar Rose were married, the
long-delayed birthday feast turning
into a splendid wedding that went on for seven
whole days and nights.

The King invited his relatives, his friends, and the nobility
from all the kingdoms near and far, or at least he invited the
sons and daughters of their sons and daughters, for all the
people that he and the Queen had known were long dead. He
also thought it prudent to send invitations to the thirteen Wise
Fairies, though only twelve of them chose to attend.

As for the prince and Briar Rose, they lived in contentment
all the rest of their days, as if—they often said—they had met
and married within the longest and most beautiful of dreams.

Illustrator's Note

When I was a girl, a thick volume of *Grimm's Fairy Tales* was my companion for many a rainy afternoon. The world of faraway kingdoms filled with princes and princesses, talking animals and magical events, held a great fascination for me. I have always been able to create vivid pictures in my mind when I read a story, and now I am lucky enough to be able to make these imaginary pictures into paintings for books.

Because I wanted the people in the book to look as if they actually lived and breathed, I sought out models who embodied as closely as possible my ideal conceptions of the characters. (Often, though, I had to greatly exaggerate a model's features to get the effect I wanted.) After having costumes made for all the characters, I took photographs, and, consulting these photographs and other reference materials (books on castles, etc.), I drew sketches for the entire book. Then I painted the illustrations in oils on stretched canvas. All the paintings are about three times the size of the printed illustrations. I work on this larger scale because I enjoy adding many details to the pictures, and because they look even sharper when reduced.

When I am working on a book I like to look at the work of other artists for inspiration. In the case of the romantic *The Sleeping Beauty,* I studied the work of the English Pre-Raphaelites, especially Waterhouse and Burne-Jones.

R.S.

A NOTE ON THE TYPE

The text of this book was set in a digitized version of Garamond No. 3, a modern rendering of the type first cut by Claude Garamond (c. 1480–1561). Garamond was a pupil of Geoffroy Tory and is believed to have based his letters on the Venetian models, although he introduced a number of important differences, and it is to him we owe the letter which we know as "old style." He gave to his letters a certain elegance and a feeling of movement that won for their creator an immediate reputation and the patronage of Francis I of France.

Composed by The Type Shop, New York, New York.

Separations, printing, and binding by Officine Grafiche di Verona, Arnoldo Mondadori Editore, Verona, Italy.

Art Direction by Armand Eisen and Thomas Durwood
Design by Ruth Sanderson
Typography and binding design by Marysarah Quinn